This book belongs to:

....

....

For Arno and Penelope, the sparkling stars
in my heart – Virginie Zurcher

For Ben, I know you'll reach the stars
one day! – Daniel Howarth

Editor: Ruth Symons
Designer: Anna Lubecka

© 2014 Quarto Publishing plc
The Old Brewery, 6 Blundell Street,
London N7 9BH, United Kingdom.
T (0)20 7700 6700 F (0)20 7700 8066
www.QuartoKnows.com

A catalogue record for this book is available from
the British Library.

ISBN: 978 1 78171 915 2

Manufactured in Shenzhen, China PP062019

19 18 17 16 15 14 13 12 11

MIX
Paper from
responsible sources
FSC® C001701
FSC
www.fsc.org

The Star of the Zoo

Virginie Zurcher

Daniel Howarth

NEW BURLINGTON

Little Star twinkled like a diamond in the clear night sky.
Far below her, the zoo was still and quiet.

The animals were getting ready for bed.

Then suddenly…

Little Star lost her balance and tumbled out of the sky!

Down,
down,
down
she
fell,
like a
shooting
star.

She left a sparkling trail all the way to the ground.

"Ouch!" she cried
as she landed with
a bump.

All the animals ran to
see what had happened.

"Oh no! Are you alright, Little Star?" asked Zebra. "Can we help you?"

"I need to get back into the sky so I can twinkle like a diamond," Little Star said sadly.

"I'll help you," said Lion. "I'm the strongest animal in the zoo."

Lion picked up Little Star, climbed onto a rock, and lifted her high into the air.

Lion could lift Little Star easily, but he couldn't reach the sky.

"I can help!" called Ant.

"Rahahaha," laughed Lion, "you're too small. You can't help."

"I'll help you," said Monkey. "I'm the best climber in the zoo."

Monkey picked up Little Star and jumped into a tree. He swung through the branches to the very top.

Monkey climbed as high as he could, but he couldn't reach the sky.

"I have a plan!" called Ant.

"Hoohoohaha," laughed Monkey, "you're too small. You can't help."

"I'll help you," said Giraffe. "I'm the tallest animal in the zoo."

Giraffe picked up Little Star, stood up straight, and stretched her neck as far as she could.

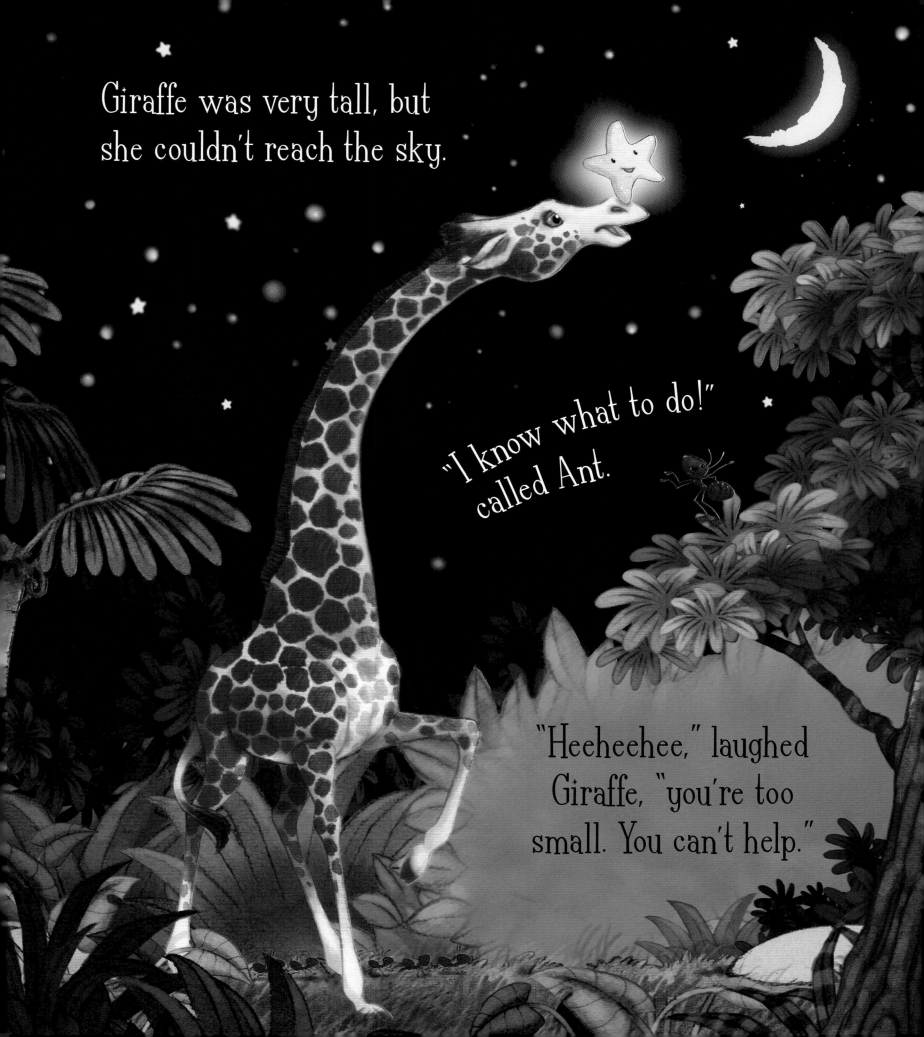

Giraffe was very tall, but
she couldn't reach the sky.

"I know what to do!"
called Ant.

"Heeheehee," laughed
Giraffe, "you're too
small. You can't help."

Little Star's
brightness
was fading.

"I have to be back in
the sky before sunrise,"
she cried.

"Give me a chance – I can help!" called Ant.

The animals all just stared at Ant. What could she do?

"Well, if you think you can do it, you might as well try," said Lion, rolling his eyes.

Ant scuttled off...

She came back, not with
ten, not with a hundred,
but with thousands
of friends to help.

Ant picked up Little Star,
and climbed onto another
ant's back.

That ant climbed
onto another ant.

And that ant climbed
onto another.

The
tower
of
ants
grew
higher
and
higher
until...

...they reached the sky!

"You did it!"
shouted Little Star.

All the animals cheered.

"Anything's possible
if you work together!"
Ant said proudly.

Little Star smiled, happy to be home.
She twinkled like a diamond all night long.

Far below, the animals finally
snuggled down and went to sleep.

Next steps

Show the children the cover and look at the book's title. Ask the children where they think the story takes place.

Ask the children if they have ever been to a zoo. What was their favourite part of the zoo and why? Do the children know where the animals in this book would live in the wild?

While reading the story, did the children predict what would happen next? Did they think that Ant would be able to help?

Discuss what it feels like to be the youngest or the smallest in a group or a class.

How did Ant and her friends help Little Star? Ask the children if they think the other animals learned anything from this. Discuss the importance of teamwork. Can the children think of a time when they achieved something with the help of their friends?

Think about the book's title. Who is the real star of the zoo? Can the children think of another good title for the story?

Ask the children to draw their favourite part of the book or their favourite zoo animal.